S0-AIH-354

Steadwell Books World Tour

CANADA

SEAN DOLAN

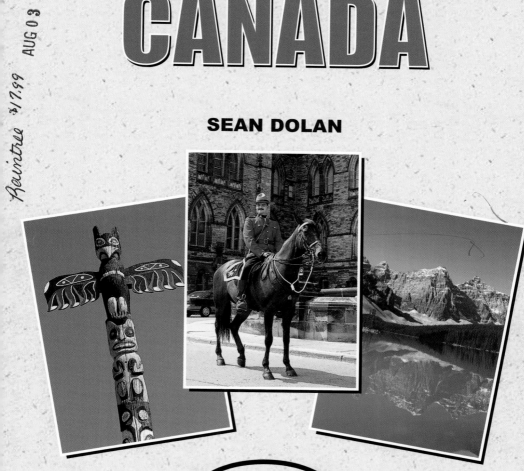

Steadwell Books

Raintree Steck-Vaughn Publishers

Harcourt Company

Austin · New York
www.raintreesteckvaughn.com

New Paris
Grade School Library

Raintree $17.99   AUG 03

Copyright © 2002 Steck-Vaughn Company

All rights reserved. No part of this book may be reproduced or utilized in any form
or by any means, electronic or mechanical, including photocopying, recording, or
by any information storage and retrieval system, without permission in writing from
the publisher. Inquiries should be addressed to: Copyright Permissions, Steck-Vaughn
Company, P.O. Box 26015, Austin, TX 78755.

Published by Raintree Steck-Vaughn Publishers,
an imprint of Steck-Vaughn Company.

Editor: Simone T. Ribke
Designer: Maria E. Torres

Library of Congress Cataloging-in-Publication Data
Dolan, Sean.
   Canada / by Leigh Ann Cobb.
      p. cm. -- (Steadwell books world tour)
   Summary: Describes the history, geography, economy, government, social life and cus-
toms, outstanding tourist sites, and more, of Canada. Includes a recipe for a Canadian
dessert.
   Includes bibliographical references and index.
   ISBN 0-7398-5533-6
      1. Canada--Juvenile literature. [1. Canada.] I. Title. II. Series.

   F1008.2 .D57 2002
   971--dc21   2002070516

Printed in the United States of America
1 2 3 4 5 6 7 8 9 10 WZ 07 06 05 04 03 02

Photo acknowledgments
Cover-a ©Bryan and Cherry Alexander; cover-b ©Hubert Stadler/CORBIS; cover-c
©Thompson Martin/ Spectrum Stock; p1a ©Spectrum Stock; p.1b ©Thompson
Martin/Spectrum Stock; p.3a ©Spectrum Stock; p.5a ©Bryan and Cherry Alexander; p.7
©Spectrum Stock; p.8 ©Bill Banaszewski/Visuals Unlimited; p.13a ©Hubert Stadler/CORBIS;
p.13b ©Thomas Kitchin/Tom Stack Associates; p.15a ©Steve Cohen/Houserstock; p.15b
©Joe Bensen/Stock Boston; p.19 ©Ottmar Bierwagen Photo Inc./ Spectrum Stock; p.21a
©Connie Colaman/Getty Images; p.21b ©Dave G. Houser/Houserstock; p.23 ©T. Kitchen/
Tom Stack & Associates; p.27a ©Mark Gibson; p.27b ©Kim Stallknecht/Spectrum Stock; p.28
©Annie Griffiths Belt/CORBIS; p.29 ©Fred Chartrand/AP/Wide World; p.31a ©Jurgen
Vogt/Getty Images; p.31b ©Robert B. McGouey/Spectrum Stock; p.33 ©Dave G.
Houser/Houserstock; p.34 ©Bill Boch/Foodpix; p.35 ©Winston Fraser; p.37 ©Galen
Rowell/CORBIS; p.38 ©Lowell Georgia/CORBIS; p.39 ©Grise Ford/SuperStock; p.40 ©Lionel
Delevingne/Stock Boston; p.41 ©Frank Scott/Spectrum Stock; p.43b ©Jean
AEF.Duboisberranger/Getty Images; p.44a,b ©Mitchell Gerber/CORBIS; p.44c ©Reuters
newMedia Inc./CORBIS;

Additional photography by Comstock, Corbis Royalty Free and Getty Royalty Free

Additional photography by PhotoDisc and Steck-Vaughn Collection.

CONTENTS

Welcome to Canada

Are you planning a trip to Canada? If so, you're bound to have fun. There is something for everyone in the world's second-largest country. Canada is a fascinating country. It has breathtaking natural beauty, friendly people, grand cities, and an unusual history. Are you ready to begin your trip? Read on.

A Tip to Get You Started

• *Use the Table of Contents*

Do you already know what you are looking for? Maybe you just want to know what topics this book will cover. The Contents page tells you what topics you will read about and where they are found in the book.

• *Look at the Pictures*

This book has lots of great photos. Flip through and check out those pictures you like the best. They will show you what the book is all about. Read the captions to learn even more about the photos.

• *Use the Glossary*

As you read this book, you may notice that some words appear in **bold** print. Look up bold words in the Glossary in the back of the book. The Glossary will help you learn what they mean.

▲ A GRAND MIDNIGHT LIGHT SHOW
The Northern Lights—also called
the Aurora Borealis—light up the
night sky over Manitoba, Canada.
Particles in the air cause this
colorful display.

POLAR BEAR ▶
A large part of Canada is too
cold for people to live in, but is
just right for animals like this
polar bear. His thick fur and a
fatty layer of blubber under his
skin help keep him warm.

CANADA'S PAST

If you are planning to visit Canada, you may want to learn about its past. Discover the story of Canada's Native American nations. Learn how the country changed once Europeans settled there. Canada's history will teach you how this country became the great nation it is today.

Ancient History

The first humans arrived in Canada 20,000 to 35,000 years ago, at the end of the last **Ice Age**. They developed into hundreds of different Native American peoples. These tribes settled across the continent and eventually developed into 12 different language groups.

The Native Americans had Canada to themselves until the 1500s. Viking sailors from Scandinavia reached Newfoundland, in eastern Canada, in the 900s. But their small **settlements** did not last long.

Permanent European settlement of Canada did not take place until the 1500s and 1600s. In the 1530s, the French sailor Jacques Cartier explored the Gulf of Saint Lawrence and the Saint Lawrence River. He became the first European to visit these sites which were important Native American trading centers. Later, these same sites became the Canadian cities of Québec and Montréal.

Cartier's discovery led France to claim and settle Canada. A Frenchman named Samuel de Champlain **founded** a settlement at Québec. He also explored the land to the west, as far as the Great Lakes and Hudson **Bay**.

A TOTEM POLE TELLS A STORY ▶
The Inuit people of western Canada carved tall totem poles out of cedar trees. Each totem (symbol) stands for a guardian animal spirit. Every Inuit clan, or family, carved its own set of totems into its totem pole.

Empire of Furs

In a short time, French fur traders were using Canada's rivers and lakes to explore the west. Canada's thick forests were home to many furry animals. These animals were trapped and killed by trappers. Their fur sold for lots of money. The coat of the beaver, in particular, was worth an enormous amount of money in Europe. People made large fortunes working in the Canadian fur trade. When the French fur traders came the Catholic **missionaries** came as well. They journeyed far into the Canadian wilderness to convert the native peoples to Catholicism, which is a form of the Christian religion.

Canada's wealth in furs drew the attention of England. English fur traders soon moved to Hudson Bay, to the north and west of the French settlements. In the 1700s, a struggle began between France and England for North American territory. This included land in what later became the United States.

▲ **WINTERLUDE IN OTTAWA**
**Skating on the Rideau Canal in Canada's capital city is fun during
the Winterlude Festival. This skating rink is the longest in the world!**

This struggle soon led to war. The French and English fought in North America between 1754 and 1763. This period is called the French and Indian War because the French combined forces with Native Americans to push England out of North America.

A.D. 1530s
Jacques Cartier explores Gulf of
St. Lawrence and St. Lawrence
River and the fur trade begins.

A.D.   0   1000   1100   1200   1300   1400   1500

A.D. 900
Vikings reach
Newfoundland.

A.D. 1500
Native American
tribes lived freely
in Canada.

8

The French and Indian War ended with England's victory and the end of French control over Canada. Many French-speaking people remained in eastern Canada, however.

The Nation of Canada

Canada became part of Great Britain. British control did not formally end until 1982. Canada's history through the 19th and 20th centuries involved adding western provinces to the original eastern settlements. The eastern provinces of Nova Scotia, New Brunswick, Québec, and Ontario were united by an act of the British Parliament in 1867. New provinces and **territories**—Manitoba, the Northwest Territories, British Columbia, Prince Edward Island, and the Yukon—were added in the late 19th century. Saskatchewan and Alberta were added in the early 20th century and Newfoundland was added in 1949.

The process of adding territories continues. The huge northern territory of Nunavut was created in 1999, and is home to much of Canada's Inuit population. Today, Canada is made up of ten provinces and three territories.

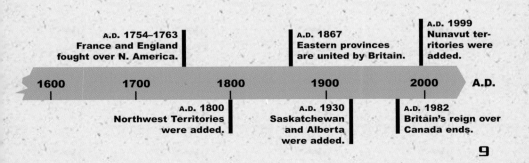

A.D. 1754–1763
France and England fought over N. America.

A.D. 1867
Eastern provinces are united by Britain.

A.D. 1999
Nunavut territories were added.

1600   1700   1800   1900   2000   A.D.

A.D. 1800
Northwest Territories were added.

A.D. 1930
Saskatchewan and Alberta were added.

A.D. 1982
Britain's reign over Canada ends.

A LOOK AT CANADA'S GEOGRAPHY

Canada is a huge country. It is much larger than the United States. In fact, Canada is the second-largest country in the world. (Russia is the largest.) Canada makes up 40% of the continent of North America.

Land

Canada is a nation of many different landscapes. From east to west Canada stretches across six different **time zones**. More than half of Canada lies above the Arctic Circle in the north. Canada's border with the United States stretches for 5,527 miles (8,895 kilometers). More than 90% of all Canadians live within 100 miles of this border.

Tall mountains line Canada in the west and the east. The Canadian Rocky Mountains ("the Rockies") in the west are the most famous. More than 30 peaks in the Rockies tower 10,000 feet (3,048 m) in height. Even so, the Torngat Range in the east is Canada's tallest mountain range.

A train trip is a great way to see Canada's many faces. Starting in the east, you'll cross dozens of waterways and rivers. In the western provinces of Saskatchewan, Manitoba, and Alberta, you'll find flat **plains** similar to the prairie lands found in the U.S. These flat plains, along with southern Ontario, are important for farming. If you travel to the north, you'll find mainly Arctic tundra. This frozen land is too cold for many people to live there.

CANADA'S SIZE ▶

Canada covers about 3,849,674 square miles (9,970,610 sq km). Water makes up a lot of this area—291,576 square miles (755,180 sq km).

▼ Below, Canada is shown as it appears on the globe.

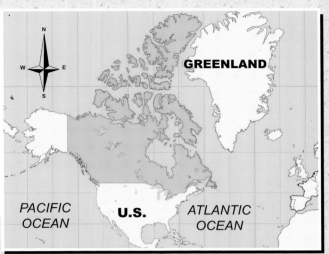

PACIFIC OCEAN

GREENLAND

U.S.

ATLANTIC OCEAN

ARCTIC OCEAN

Alaska (U.S.)

Greenland

Baffin Bay

Yukon River

Mackenzie River

Great Bear Lake

Davis Strait

CANADA

Labrador Sea

Hudson Bay

Saskatchewan River

Vancouver

Calgary

Lake Winnipeg

Québec

Montréal

Lake Superior

Ottawa

UNITED STATES

Lake Huron

Lake Ontario

Lake Michigan

Lake Erie

ATLANTIC OCEAN

CANADA

★ National Capital
● Major Cities
— Rivers

0 200 400 Kilometers
0   200   400 Miles

Water

Water has played an important part in Canada's history. Early fur trappers from Europe explored the country by boat. Many of Canada's rivers and lakes are connected, which has made it easy for people to travel long distances.

Today, the Gulf of Saint Lawrence and the Saint Lawrence River allow ships to travel easily between the east and the midwest. Most ships travel along the Saint Lawrence Seaway—it's like a giant highway for boats.

In the west, the Mackenzie, Fraser, Columbia, Klondike, and Yukon Rivers are Canada's great rivers. Hudson Bay and James Bay are the major waterways of the north, but they are less important for trade than those connected to the Saint Lawrence Seaway.

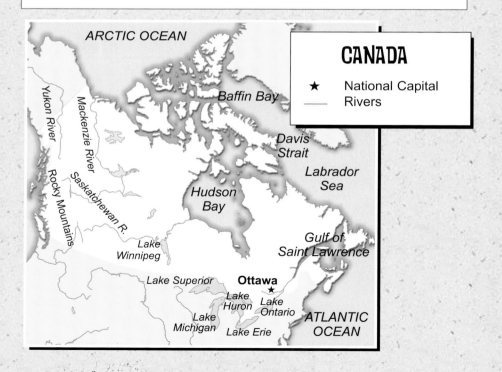

THE ROAR OF MIGHTY NIAGARA FALLS... ▶
... is background music for these visitors. If you join them, you too will be glad to wear a yellow raincoat to stay dry. Niagara Falls is on the border of the province of Ontario and New York State.

◀ LAKE SUPERIOR Lake Superior, in Ontario, is one of the five Great Lakes that forms the border between Canada and the U.S. The others are Lakes Erie, Huron, Michigan, and Ontario.

New Paris
Grade School Library

Weather

Many people think of Canada as a snowy wilderness, but that is not the case. Canada has four seasons. In the northern regions, winter can last longer than summer, spring, and fall. Average temperatures in the winter fall below freezing—32 degrees Fahrenheit (0° C). During the winter, the ground is usually covered with snow.

In general, the parts of Canada farthest from the ocean are the coldest in winter and the hottest in summer. Ontario and Québec have hot summers that follow their very cold winters. The northernmost regions have long, cold winters and short, cool summers.

The northern part of Canada is very close to the North Pole, so it is very cold. It is too cold for many people to live in. There, you will find icy **glaciers** and Arctic tundra. Be sure to bring a warm coat and good snow boots if you visit—you'll need protection from freezing winds and the ice that always covers the ground in some places!

Rain is heaviest in Ontario and Québec. Snowfall is heaviest in the Canadian Rockies and along the Gulf of Saint Lawrence.

▲ EASY LIVING ON PRINCE EDWARD ISLAND
This is one of the prettiest places to visit in Canada. In summer, you can enjoy warm weather along its beaches. Inland, Prince Edward Island is covered in lush green grass and colorful wildflowers.

ROUGH GOING IN BRITISH COLUMBIA ▶
Picking a safe path through the ice is a challenge when mountain climbing in winter. These hikers are climbing Snowpatch Sphere on Crescent Glacier in the mountains of British Columbia, Canada's western province.

TORONTO: A BIG-CITY SNAPSHOT

▲ **TORONTO HARBOR**
Skyscrapers in downtown Toronto are dwarfed by CN Tower, the world's tallest building. To its left is the Skydome arena. Take a trip to the top of CN Tower for a great view of the city and distant countryside.

Toronto is Canada's largest and most important city. It is not the nation's capital—that's Ottawa—but it's the capital of Ontario, Canada's richest province. A province is like a state in the United States. Toronto's clean streets and friendly people have led it to be called "Toronto the Good."

How Toronto Grew

Toronto lies on the north shore of Lake Ontario. This lake forms part of the border between Canada and the United States. Today's city lies on what was once an Iroquois Indian settlement. The Iroquois valued the location because it allowed easy access to land and water **trade routes**. These same routes were later used by French and English explorers, fur traders, soldiers, and missionaries.

Today, Toronto still benefits from its location. The Saint Lawrence Seaway connects Toronto by water with the Saint Lawrence River, Montréal, Québec, and the Atlantic Ocean to the east. Lake Ontario allows Toronto to trade with the U.S. cities south of the Great Lakes, such as Chicago and Detroit.

A Modern City

Toronto looks like any modern city in the U.S. It has many tall buildings, such as the Toronto–Dominion Center and the Canada Trust Tower. The tallest building in Toronto is the CN Tower. Actually, it is the tallest building in the world.

It stands 1,815 feet (553 m) high! It has become the most recognizable **symbol** of Toronto.

The CN Tower in the heart of Toronto's business district is the perfect place to begin your tour of Toronto. Just a short walk away is the Toronto Stock Exchange, Canada's Wall Street. If you are there on a weekday, stop in and watch the traders in action. Nearby, "Mint Corner" is home to Canada's largest banks.

Now that you've seen where Toronto makes and keeps its money, make your way to the city's beautiful waterfront on Lake Ontario. Visit one of the many restaurants along the waterfront's quays (docks). Watch the distant ships on Lake Ontario and the boats close up in its harbor. Ride a ferry boat across to the Toronto Islands.

Are you ready for some shopping yet? Say goodbye to the waterfront and head downtown. Yonge Street is the site of every kind of shop you can imagine—clothes, souvenirs, electronics, local crafts—and plenty of restaurants. The Saint Lawrence Market is a great place to shop for all kinds of fresh food, especially fish, fresh fruits, and vegetables.

When you are through shopping, step into Saint James Cathedral for calm and beauty. A pretty park surrounds it.

Evening is the perfect time to visit Toronto's Chinatown. It has many restaurants, shops, art galleries, and fantastic Chinese food.

TORONTO'S OLDEST RESIDENTS? ▶
The Royal Ontario Museum in Toronto has fascinating exhibits, including these dinosaur bones from ages past.

TORONTO'S TOP-10 CHECKLIST

If your trip to Canada includes a stop in Toronto, here's a list of 10 things you should try to do.

☐ Tour the CN Tower, the tallest building in the world.

☐ Take the ferry to the Toronto Islands.

☐ Watch the busy trading on the floor of the Toronto Stock Exchange, Canada's Wall Street.

☐ Shop for cool clothes in the stores on Yonge Street.

☐ Marvel at the high-flying feats of Vince Carter, star of the Toronto Raptors basketball team.

☐ Visit Maple Leaf Gardens, home of one of the original teams in the National Hockey League.

☐ Spend the day shopping and eating in Chinatown.

☐ Enjoy a performance by the Toronto Symphony Orchestra.

☐ Wander the fairgrounds during the annual late-summer Canadian National Exhibition, which features an air show, live theatre and music, and much more!

☐ Watch the boats and the day pass by on the Lake Ontario waterfront.

4 TOP SIGHTS

Montréal and Québec

No trip to Canada is complete without a visit to the province of Québec and its two largest cities, Montréal and Québec City. In the province of Québec, people speak French.

Montréal is the largest French-speaking city. But you'll still find it easy to get around even if you only speak English. Montréal was built on an island in the Saint Lawrence River. It was originally a center of Canada's fur trade and also of the Roman Catholic Church in America.

Mont Royal (Royal Mountain) towers over Montréal and gives the city its name. Montréal is famous for its stylish restaurants and clubs. Young visitors will especially enjoy attractions such as the Biodome. The Biodome has an indoor tropical forest, where you can explore tropical animals and plants no matter what the weather outside. There is also a mountain landscape and a polar habitat, where you can see what animals live in the Arctic parts of Canada. You can also discover what lives in and around the Saint Lawrence River at the marine ecosystem.

In Québec City, the French influence is even more obvious. Québec is the capital of the province and is Canada's oldest city.

Just outside the city, visit the Plains of Abraham. This is where the French were finally defeated in the French and Indian War. The nearby Laurentian Mountains are a great site for skiing and other winter sports.

▼ THE CATHEDRAL OF MONTRÉAL
Built between 1870 and 1894, this grand church serves Montréal's large Roman Catholic population.

LIFESTYLES OF THE BIODOME ▶
The Biodome is an environmental museum in Montréal. Inside, you can visit four different ecosystems, or life environments. When it's freezing outside, try a visit to the warm tropics of the Biodome.

Vancouver

Vancouver is a city in the western province of British Columbia. It is Canada's "gateway to the Pacific." This city is the center of Canada's trade with Asia. Tucked between mountains and the Pacific Ocean, it is also one of the most beautiful cities in the world.

While in Vancouver, be sure to check out Gastown. It offers a re-creation of old Vancouver. There you can see how Vancouver looked back in the 19th century.

Stanley Park covers more than 1,000 acres near the entry to Vancouver's stunning harbor. It includes gardens, an **arboretum**, a zoo, and a world-famous aquarium. Home to a large population of Asian **immigrants**, Vancouver is also well known for its Chinatown.

Vancouver is a great place for those who love the outdoors. With a large portion of Vancouver lying right on a bay, you can enjoy swimming, sailing, and sunbathing on the many beaches. Kayaking and rowing are also very popular. There are many places to rent equipment and even take lessons. Also, you might want to bring your binoculars—the waters around Vancouver offer the best locations for whale watching.

If you prefer trees to sand, you'll love Vancouver. Thick forests cover mountains outside the city. They offer many nature and hiking trails, your chance to see woodland wildlife.

▲ FALSE CREEK MARINA
The marina is the place to dock your boat when sailing into Vancouver, in far western Canada. It's fun to wander among the nearby stores and market before you explore the city.

▼ MORAINE LAKE
Its beautiful turquoise (bright blue-green) color has given Moraine Lake its nickname: "Jewel of the Rockies."

FASCINATING FACT

The great elk, or Wapiti, can be found high in the Rocky Mountains...or just walking through town! In September, the males gather near Banff National Park. They compete for females by locking horns. This means they charge at each other, heads down, with their antlers, making a huge crashing sound. The winner gets the girl.

The elk sometimes attack cars. They mistake a car for another elk and may try to lock horns with your bumper. So if you visit Banff during this time, steer clear of the elk!

Vancouver is one of the most bicycle-friendly cities in the world. Perhaps you'd like to explore the city on a rented bicycle. People from Vancouver pride themselves on being athletic and in good shape. You are sure to be inspired by so many runners in the parks and on the sidewalks—so bring your running shoes and shorts!

The Canadian Rockies

The Canadian Rocky Mountain range is one of the great natural wonders of the world. The Canadian Rockies border the provinces of British Columbia and Alberta. The most spectacular parts are preserved in two national parks, Banff and Jasper.

Banff National Park is the southernmost park. It is most popular with tourists. Banff was Canada's first official **wildlife sanctuary**. It is Canada's most popular resort spot in both the summer and winter. One of the highlights of the park is Moraine Lake. Formed by glaciers, Moraine Lake is famous for the bright blue color of its waters.

Jasper National Park is also beautiful. It is a little wilder than Banff. The Columbia Icefield connects the two parks. It is made up of 30 glaciers from the last Ice Age.

These parks are home to many different kinds of wildlife. There are grizzly bears, elk, and antelope. Be sure to watch out for cougars, wolves, and bighorn sheep, too. Bring your camera in case you come face to face with one of these animals. But do not expect to see all of the animals at once.

The Calgary Stampede

Each year in the first and second weeks of July, the city of Calgary in Alberta hosts the Calgary Stampede. The Calgary Stampede is the world's biggest rodeo. Many call it "the greatest outdoor show on Earth."

Calgary is the center of Canada's cattle-ranching industry. When you visit, be prepared to see real-life cowboys and cowgirls—you'll want a camera here. The Calgary Stampede celebrates the cowboy's way of life.

The Stampede begins with a huge parade through downtown Calgary. Each day, the rodeo holds competitions in traditional cowboy events. These include bronco-busting (riding a wild horse), lasso (or rope) throwing, and steer wrestling. The chuckwagon races are especially popular. You'll know the chuckwagon races have started when you see a bunch of horses pulling wagons around a race track—as fast as they can go.

At night at the Stampede, you can walk through the midway, visiting the exhibition halls and stalls where Canada's finest **stock breeders** show off prize cattle and horses. There is an awesome fireworks show every night as well as musical performances.

A special kids' area is like a huge amusement park. There are rides and visits by cartoon characters and television favorites. You can buy a cowboy hat and a lasso, or maybe a Native American headdress.

COWBOYS AT THE CORRAL ▶
These real-life cowboys are
checking their schedule for
the next event at the Calgary
Stampede, "the greatest
outdoor show on Earth." They
won't stay this clean for long.

▲ CHUCKWAGON RACES
Chuckwagon racing is one of the most exciting
events at the Calgary Stampede. Only a skilled
driver can keep ahead of the pack—and out
of the way of danger.

GOING TO SCHOOL IN CANADA

Each province in Canada has its own way of running its public schools. Québec, for example, tries to preserve its French culture. Classes there are taught in French. In the other provinces, most classes are taught in English.

Most Canadian children attend one year of kindergarten, eight years of elementary school, and four years of high school. The subjects taught are generally the same as in schools in the United States. Almost all Canadians can read and write.

A large percentage of Canadian students go on to college. Most of Canada's universities are **funded** by the governments of the individual provinces.

▲ SHHH... BRAINS WORKING
These two students are hard at work in a Canadian classroom.

Canadians enjoy many different sports. There are Major League Baseball teams in Toronto and Montréal. There is a National Basketball Association team in Toronto. Canada also has a professional football league, the CFL (Canadian Football League).

Canada's official national game is lacrosse (lah-CROSS). Players use sticks that have a small net on the top to pass around a small, hard ball on an outdoor field. Lacrosse is actually a Native American game. It was played long before the Europeans came to Canada!

Ice hockey is one of the most popular sports in Canada. Canadians invented hockey as a winter sport. They played it on frozen lakes, rivers, and ponds. Teams from Canadian cities play in the National Hockey League (NHL). Ice hockey is also very much a small-town sport in Canada. Hundreds of towns support teams and players in junior leagues.

FOLLOW THAT PUCK! ▶
Many Canadians take hockey very seriously. Thousands pack the stands at local and provincial games to cheer on their favorite teams.

FROM FARMING TO FACTORIES

Canada began as a major **supplier** of fur. Traders shipped furs back to Europe to be used for clothing. Huge fur-trapping companies became successful.

The most important parts of Canada's present economy are manufacturing and services. In manufacturing, the iron and steel **industries** are especially important. They produce parts for automobiles, mining equipment, and household appliances. Canada also **exports** oil and natural gas to countries around the world.

Mining and farming are important, but not as much as they used to be. Canada produces much of the world's grain, especially wheat. But less than 5% of Canadian land can be used for farming.

More than 54% of Canada is covered with forests. These forests are used for logging, or cutting down trees, which is used to make wood products.

The fishing industry is largest near Hudson Bay and in the northwest near the Pacific Ocean. Working in the fishing industry is another way Canadians earn a living. The kind of money Canadians use is called the Canadian dollar.

The largest part of the Canadian economy is the service industry. The jobs that people do in the service industry provide services to people, such as transportation, tourism (especially camping, hunting, and fishing), food, recreation, hotels, and housing. So some Canadians may work as phone operators, bus drivers, cooks, or travel agents. Because Canada is so large, transportation is especially important, to residents and tourists alike.

LOGGING ▶
Powerful machine jaws assist loggers in stacking the logs after the trees have been cut down with the aid of huge powered saws. Logging is a very important industry in Canada.

◀ ON THE ROAD AGAIN
Many Canadians love to travel, especially within Canada. Campers and RVs (recreational vehicles) are a popular way to explore this huge country.

THE CANADIAN GOVERNMENT

Canada is a parliamentary democracy. It has ten provinces and three territories. Each is represented in Parliament. Everyone in Canada above the age of 18 has the right to vote.

Parliament consists of two houses, or parts. The lower house of Parliament is the House of Commons. The upper house is known as the Senate. The governments of the different provinces appoint the Senate's 104 senators.

The head of the government is the prime minister. The prime minister chooses advisers to be members of his or her Cabinet. Although Canada governs itself, the official head of state remains the queen or king of England.

CANADA'S NATIONAL FLAG

The Canadian flag, also called The Maple Leaf flag, was adopted in 1964. The red and white colors are the national colors of Canada. Until 1860, the national symbol was the beaver but in that year the maple leaf became popular and has been the national emblem ever since. Canada is known for its maple trees which produce wonderful pure maple syrup.

RELIGIONS OF CANADA

People in Canada come from many different places. They follow a wide variety of religions. Most, however, are Christian. More than 46% of Canadians are Roman Catholics. Catholics observe the teachings of Jesus as written in the New Testament of the Bible. The head of the Roman Catholic Church is the Pope, who lives near Rome in Italy. About 36% of Canadians are Protestant. Protestants are also Christians, but have no special leader like the Pope.

Many Canadians follow other religions as well. Some are Buddhist, Hindu, or Sikh. Others are Jewish or Muslim. In fact, more than 1% of Canadians are Jewish. There are very large Jewish communities in both Toronto and Montréal. Muslims, Buddhists, Hindus, Sikhs, and followers of Native American religions represent about 3% of the people in Canada.

NOTRE DAME BASILICA ▶
This early cathedral,
completed in 1829,
is in Montréal.

CANADIAN FOOD

Canadian food varies greatly depending on where in Canada you are. In Ontario, for example, much of the food you find will be similar to what you find in England, or even in the United States. In Québec, the food is much more likely to have a French flavor.

In cities like Vancouver and Toronto, you will find food from many different cultures, such as Chinese or Korean food.

Fish is an important part of the diet in the eastern provinces. That is because of all the fishing done on the nearby waters.

A popular Canadian meal is the "logger's breakfast." This comes from the eastern provinces. A logger's breakfast is pancakes topped with maple syrup with a serving of trempetti (bread soaked in maple syrup and topped with cream) on the side.

◀ **MMMM... MAPLE SYRUP**
The sweetness of maple syrup, boiled down from many gallons of the sap of the maple tree, was popular with Native Americans in Canada long before the Europeans came. It remains so popular today that there is even a maple leaf on the Canadian flag!

Canada's Recipe

NANAIMO BARS

Ingredients:

For the bottom layer:
1 cup melted butter (2 sticks)
1/2 cup granulated sugar
1 cup cocoa
2 eggs
3 cups graham cracker crumbs
1 1/2 cups flaked coconut
1 cup chopped walnuts

For the middle layer:
1/2 cup butter
4 tbsp custard powder
2 tbsp vanilla
3 tbsp of milk
2 cups powdered sugar

For icing:
8 ounces semi-sweet chocolate
4 ounces unsweetened chocolate
3 1/2 tbsp butter

WARNING:
Never cook or bake by yourself. Always have an adult assist you in the kitchen.

Directions:

To make the bottom layer: Mix together the melted butter and sugar. Add the cocoa, then the eggs. Beat until smooth. Add graham cracker crumbs and mix thoroughly. Mix in coconut and walnuts. Press into two 9-inch pans. Put in refrigerator.

To make the middle layer: Cream together the butter, the custard powder, and the vanilla. Gradually blend in milk and powdered sugar. Spread evenly over base. Chill well before icing.

To make the icing: Melt chocolate and butter together on low heat. Spread onto chilled middle layer. Chill in refrigerator. Cut into pieces or bars before the chocolate on top has completely hardened. Store in the refrigerator.

UP CLOSE: NUNAVUT

Nunavut (NOO-na-voot) is Canada's newest territory. It was formed by the division of some of Canada's Northwest Territories. It became part of the Canadian **federation** in 1999.

Nunavut may be large, but very few people live there—only about 27,000 people. Fewer people live in this region than in any other in Canada. Nunavut measures almost 800,000 square miles (2 million sq km). It makes up one-fifth of all of Canada's land.

Most of the people who live in Nunavut are Inuit (IN-yoo-it). The Inuit are the native people of northern Canada, Greenland, and Alaska. Outside of Canada, Inuit are sometimes called Eskimos. However, people don't like to use the word "Eskimo" anymore. They use the word "Inuit," which means "the people" in Inuktitut. Inuktitut is the language of the Inuit people.

Nunavut was born from a lawsuit filed by the Inuit against the government of Canada. The Inuit were suing for the return of their traditional lands. Non-Inuit people are free to live in Nunavut, but the Inuit govern the territory. The word Nunavut means "our land."

Life in Nunavut is very different from life in most other places in Canada. Nunavut is an Arctic region. It has a harsh, cold climate and spectacular natural beauty. Its landscape includes tundra, lakes, mountain ranges, icebergs, and even glaciers. Tundra is a flat, cold area with few trees. Settlements are small and very far apart.

▲ BAFFIN ISLAND, IN NUNAVUT
Icy cold for most of the year, Baffin Island melts
into a beautiful green landscape in the summer.

▼ WHALING

The Inuit people once depended on whale meat to survive. These Inuit villagers are butchering a bowhead whale. The Inuit are respectful of the whales and are careful not to take too many.

Even the capital city, Iqaluit, has a population of only 4,500 people. In most towns, the landing strip for airplanes is their lifeline and link to the rest of Canada.

The "Nunavut automobile" is a four-wheeled all-terrain vehicle (ATV). An ATV can run on all kinds of ground and in even the most rugged weather. Today's Inuit often ride ATVs to traditional hunting grounds. In winter, which can last from November through April, the snowmobile is the best way to get around because there is so much snow and ice.

The people who live in Nunavut do things like watch television (from satellite dishes), use personal computers, and drive snowmobiles, trucks, and ATVs. However, many also hunt caribou, seals, walrus, whales, fish, and even polar bears. They use the meat and furs to feed and clothe their families. Most Inuit believe that having their own territory gives them the best chance of keeping their culture and customs so that they can last far into the future.

SNOWMOBILES! ▶
In many parts of Nunavut a snowmobile is the best way to get around. Ice and snow make the ground too slippery for cars or trucks.

HOLIDAYS

Canadian Holidays

Canada celebrates several national holidays. Perhaps the most important is Canada Day, which falls on July 1. Canada Day is like Independence Day in the United States. It honors the day when the Canadian provinces united and became Canada.

Victoria Day is celebrated on the Monday preceding May 25. It honors Queen Victoria's birthday. She ruled Great Britain from 1837 to 1901.

Canadian Thanksgiving is celebrated on the second Monday of October. Canada also celebrates Remembrance Day on November 11 in honor of its soldiers killed in World War I and other conflicts. Canada also celebrates Christmas, Easter, New Year's Day, and Labor Day.

▲ CANADA DAY
Families and friends get together to celebrate being Canadian, with parades, music, good food, and fun.

LEARNING THE LANGUAGE

English	French	How to say it
Hello	Bonjour	bon-JHOOR
Good bye	Au revoir	OH rev-WAHR
How are you	Comment allez-vous?	KOH-munt AH-lay VOO
My name is	Je m'appelle	JHEH mah-PELL
Please	S'il vous plaît	SEE VOO PLAY
Thank you	Merci	mehr-SEE
Excuse me	Excusez-moi	ek-SKOO-say MWAH

QUICK FACTS

CANADA

Capital ▶
Ottawa, Ontario

Borders
United States (S)
Greenland (NE)
Pacific Ocean (W)
Atlantic Ocean (E)

Area
3,851,788 square miles
(9,976 sq km)

Population
31,902,268

Chief Crops
Wheat, barley, oilseed, tobacco,
fruits, vegetables, dairy products,
forest products, fish

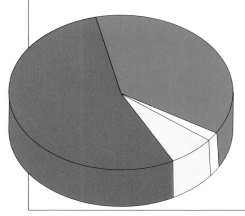

Largest Cities
Toronto (4,263,757 people)
Montréal (3,326,510)
Vancouver (1,831,665)
Ottawa (1,010,498)

◀ **Main Religious Groups**

46% Roman Catholicism
36% Protestantism
17% other
1% Judaism

▲ Flag of Canada

Coastline
125,570 miles (202,080 km)

Longest River ▶
Yukon River
1,979 miles (3,185 km)

Literacy Rate
96% of all Canadians
can read

Major Industries
Processed and unprocessed
minerals, food products,
wood and paper products,
transportation equipment,
chemicals, fish products,
petroleum, and natural gas

Natural Resources
Iron ore, nickel, zinc, copper, gold,
molybdenum, potash, silver, fish,
timber, wildlife, natural gas,
hydropower, petroleum

◀ **Monetary Unit**
Canadian dollar

PEOPLE TO KNOW

◀ MIKE MYERS

Mike Myers is just one of several famous Canadian comedians. Born in Toronto in 1963, his fame began when he joined the cast of the TV program *Saturday Night Live* in 1989. From there he branched out into movies, which include *Austin Powers* and *Wayne's World*.

SHANIA TWAIN ▶

Shania Twain was born in 1965 and grew up in Ontario, Canada. After losing both parents in a car accident, Twain raised her younger brothers and sister. Twain's music breakthrough came in 1996 with her second album, which spent 100 weeks on the charts. It is the best-selling country music album of all time.

◀ WAYNE GRETZKY

Hockey is Canada's favorite sport, and Wayne Gretzky is hockey's greatest player of all time. In his 20-year career, which ended in 1999, Gretzky set more than 60 National Hockey League records. On the ice, Gretzky was known for his skill. Off the ice, Gretzky is loved by Canadians for being a great guy. He was born in 1961.

MORE TO READ

**Do you want to know more about Canada?
Check out the books below.**

Allison, R. J. *Country Fact Files: Canada*. New York, NY: Raintree Steck-Vaughn Publishers, 1996.

Learn all about the landscape, climate, natural resources, culture, and industry of Canada.

Darlington, Robert A. *Nations of the World: Canada*. New York, NY: Raintree Steck-Vaughn Publishers, 2000.

Explore the nation of Canada through its history, people, lifestyles, landscape and cities.

Park, Ted. *Taking Your Camera to Canada*. New York, NY: Raintree Steck-Vaughn Publishers, 2001.

Explore the great country of Canada from behind the lens of a camera.

Kramer, Sydelle A. *The Great Gretzky*. New York, NY: Penguin Putnam Books for Young Readers, 1999.

Wayne Gretzky is one of the greatest hockey players of all time. Learn all the details of this great sportsman's life in this fact-filled biography.

GLOSSARY

Arboretum (ahr-boh-REE-tum)—a place where special trees are grown

Bay (BAY)—a crescent-shaped body of water, which can be small or very large

Clan (KLAN)—a large family group that includes aunts, uncles, cousins, and many generations

Continent (KAHN-tih-nent)—one of six huge land masses on Earth: Antarctica, Asia, Australia, Europe, North America, and South America

Exported (EKS-por-ted)—sent to another country for selling purposes

Federation (fed-er-AY-shun)—a group of states that have joined together under one government

Founded (FOWN-ded)—set up in the beginning (like a store or a country)

Funded (FUN-ded)—gave money to

Glaciers (GLAY-sherz)—huge ice masses in the form of rivers that are found around the North and South Poles

Ice Age (ICE AGE)—a time when the Earth's climate was so much cooler that ice covered most of the continents; there have been several Ice Ages since Earth was formed.

Immigrants (IM-ih-gruhnts)—people who have come from a different country to settle in a new country

Industries (IN-duss-treez)—large businesses with many people working on different kinds of jobs

Missionaries (MISH-uhn-air-eez)—people sent out to different regions or countries to tell the people there about their own church's beliefs

Plains (PLAYNZ)—wide areas of land with few trees, usually grassy

Settlement (SET-uhl-ment)—the town created by a group of people in a new place

Stock breeders (STAHK BREE-derz)—people who raise cows, horses, pigs, sheep, or other animals in large numbers

Supplier (suh-PLY-er)—someone who gives or sells things that other people need

Symbol (SIM-buhl)—a picture or object that represents something else

Territories (TAIR-ih-tore-eez)—large divisions of a country where not many people live

Time zones (TIME ZOHNZ)—sections of the Earth where everybody sets their clocks to the same time

Trade routes (TRAYD ROOTS)—the paths taken by people on land or sea to bring goods from one country or area to another for sale or trade

Wildlife sanctuary (WILD-life SANG-choo-air-ee)—a place where animals, birds, and fish are protected from hunting or destruction

INDEX